The Book of Spiritual Solution

He, She and The Tree

The 12 Sun Concept

Duane A. Garrett, Sr.

The Book of Spiritual Solution:
He, She and The Tree

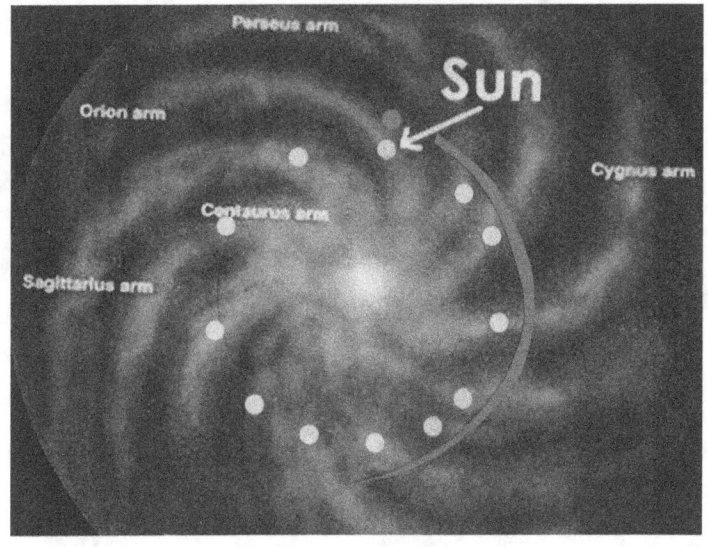

The 12 Sun Concept

ReadersMagnet, LLC

The Book of Spiritual Solution: He, She and the Tree.
Copyright © 2022 by Duane A. Garrett, Sr.

Published in the United States of America.
ISBN   Paperback: 978-1-955603-68-3
ISBN   eBook: 978-1-955603-67-6

All rights reserved. No part of this publication may be reproduced, stored in a retrieval system or transmitted in any way by any means, electronic, mechanical, photocopy, recording or otherwise without the prior permission of the authorexcept as provided by USA copyright law.

The opinions expressed by the author are not necessarily those of ReadersMagnet, LLC.

ReadersMagnet, LLC
10620 Treena Street, Suite 230 | San Diego, California, 92131 USA
1.619. 354. 2643 | www.readersmagnet.com

Book design copyright © 2022 by ReadersMagnet, LLC. All rights reserved.
Cover design by Ericka Obando
Interior design by Mary Mae Romero

Contents

IY(eye)AM 1

Great Seal 2

Archer 4

Scorpion 6

Scales 8

Virgin 10

Lion 12

Crab 14

Twins 16

Bull 18

Ram 20

2-Fish 22

Water Bearer 24

Eye of Infinity 26

Dedication

This book is dedicated to "Infinity", the Father and Mother,
the He and She of our existence, here on Earth and
in Heaven and to all the Mothers throughout time who
have not been given the proper Respect due all Mothers.
This book is intended to put Woman back
on the Pedestal of Life and Light.
Forgive us Mother, for forgetting about you
especially when we scream your name at birth. (Y)

This Version of Creation contains no talking snake, no hell
and No Devil. Just D-Evil that man does to control people.

For Doris Garrett,

The first Mother, Teacher, Counselor, and Best Friend
I ever had. I owe you my life and will be forever grateful.

Introduction

This is a 12-step Spiritual Guide to lead the
Children of the Third and Fourth Generation out of the
Darkness and back to the Understanding of the Living Light.

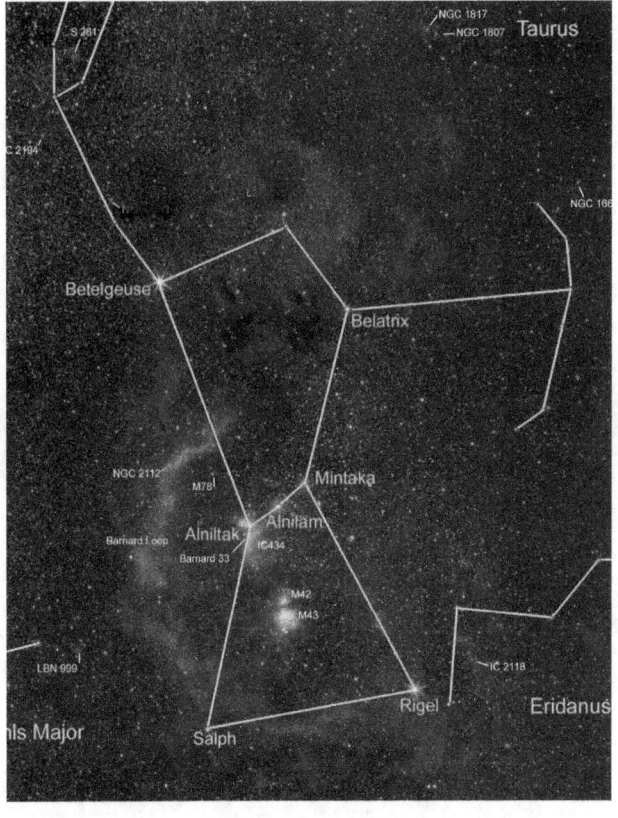

Peace on Earth with the Tree of Life
The Constellation Itym
None are so blind than he who will no See

THE WISDOM OF THE AGES
The Greatest Never Ending Story Ever Told
12 Constellations in This Story

Great Seal	Cosmic Force of Creation
Archer	Life Force of Man
Scorpion	Death of Man
Scales	Judgment of Man
Virgin Lily	Immaculate Conception & Resurrection of Man
Lion	A New Kings Birth One Land One King
Crab	Great Flood
Twins of	Gin & Isys Shiva & Shiba
The Apis Bull	Osiris and Isys
The Ram	Akhenaten & Tiye Ramses & Moses
The 2-Fish	Jesus & Miry
The Water Bearer	CAPT Amiryca Cultural Awareness Program & Training

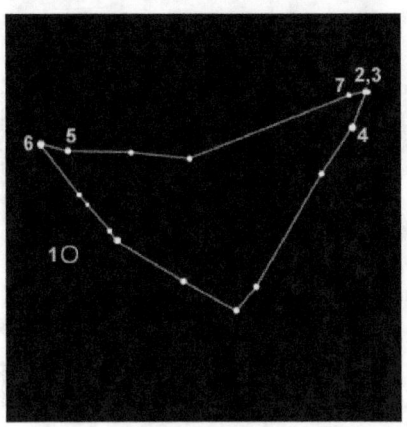

IY(eye)AM

Before the beginning **& After** the end of time, there will always be "**Infinity**". A **Vortex of Ever Living Light** but **This Light** is like no other Light. **This Light** is so bright and so intense that nothing can escape **This Light** not even darkness. And when nothing existed **This Light** did. Within the center of this **Ever-Living Light of Love** exist **2** consciousness, **2** intelligences that lives as **One**, with the greatest of understanding that **"One cannot exist without the other" (First Uni-Verse).** They are the beginning and the end of all thought, all things and each other. These **2** inseparable forces are the "**I**" & the "**Y**" that makes up **Infinity**, a force that has no beginning and no end. Where **He & She are One**, Father Time & Mother Nature, **IY(eye)AM** both but neither and **IY(eye)AM Home** for all spirits terrestrial and extraterrestrial, now and forever. Then a thought came out of this **Living Light of Love** like a soft and gentle voice saying "Let there be a Light" and then there was a Light, the **First Sun** of This **Ever-Living Light** was created.

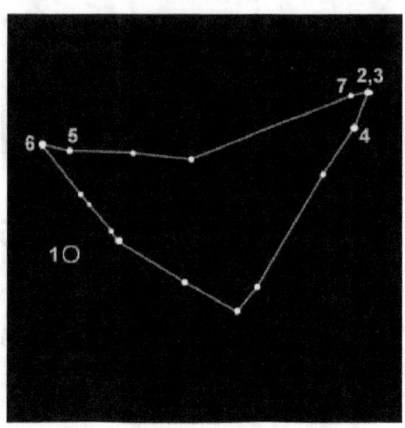

Great Seal

IY said "This day shall be forever known as (fka) "**Sunday**"(**Sun day**). Remember it as the **First day** of Time, the day **IY** created Our **Sun**. The morning of the **2nd day, IY** said "Let us pull a blanket of darkness over our Sun so that he may sleep". So **IY** called forth the darkness creating A **Moon** to Set and to rule in the night sky while our **Sun(Set)** sleeps. **IY** said "This day shall be forever known as (fka) "**Monday**" (**Moon Day**). Remember it as the **2nd day** of Time, the day **IY** created Our **Moon**. And on the morning of the **3rd day**, **IY** said "Let us make them in our image and in our likeness, standing equal in mind and spirit, opposite only in flesh". **IY** then commanded atom to grow creating the **Earth** and Universes of **12 Suns** along with all things big and small. And from the dust of this **Earth, IY** created the **2(He & She)** in our image and in our likeness. **IY** created the He and the She; both male and female calling them **Itym & Ivy**. **IY** said " This day shall be forever known as (fka) "**Tuesday**"(**2's day)**.

The Book of Spiritual Solution: He, She and the Tree

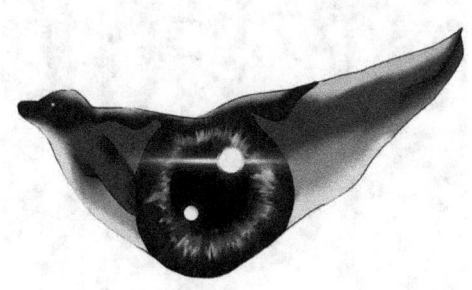

Remember it as the **3rd day** of Time, the day **IY** created the **2(He and She)** from the dust of this "**Earth**". On the morning of the **4th day**, **IY** said "Let us gathered together the **4 Winds** of Time" creating a **Great Mountain**. And atop this **Great Mountain**, **IY** placed **He, She and the very First Tree**. Blowing into them the **Breath of Life** and the Cosmic Consciousness of the **I** & the **Y** giving them Life and the wisdom of the Uni-Verse that "**One cannot live without the other**". **IY** then said "This day shall be forever known as (fka) "**Wednesday**".(**Winds Day**). Remember it as the **4th day** of Time, the day **IY** gathered together the "**4 Winds**" and blew into you the **Breath of Life**. The morning of the **5th day**, this Earth was a dry wasteland devoid of life and He, She and the Tree grew Thirsty. **IY** said "Let us bring forth **Water** to this dry and desolate land". So **IY** commanded our Sun to melt the polar caps of this Earth then commanding the 4 Winds to bring them **Water** to drink; so He, She and the Tree will thirst no more, **IY** then said "This day shall be forever known as (fka)"**Thursday**"(**Thirst Day**).

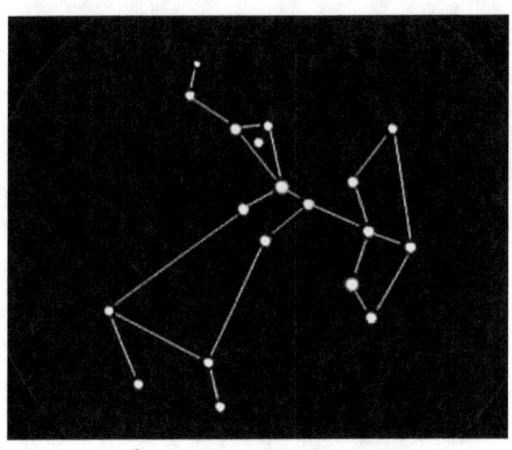

Archer

Remember it as the **5th day** of Time, the day **IY** created "**Water**". On the morning of the **6th day**, the waters continued to rise. **IY** said "Let there be another Light, a **2nd Sun(Rise)**. She shall be a companion to our **Sun(Set)** in this time of change and to calm the raging seas. **IY** then sent a **2nd Sun(Rise)** to make **2 Great Lights** in the sky and to keep Our 12 Suns in order and when She came, **She brought** the **Lightning**, She brought the **Thunder**, the ground begin to move. It started raining down rocks from the sky dragging **Fire**. The raging seas became calm. The water began to recede **IY** said "This day shall be forever known as(fka) "**Friday**"(**Fried Day**) the day the earth is fried from the rocks falling from the skies dragging **Fire**. IY said "Remember This Day as the **6th day** of Time, the day **IY** created "**Fire**". Then came the morning of the **7th day**, as **He and She sat in the Tree** holding onto its **branches** for protection. They **sat and watch** the waters recede uncovering the "**First Super Iyland**". They **sat and watched** as these **Twin Suns** give New Life to This Earth like a Mother to a child.

Giving Honor to our **Sun(Set)** as "**Father**" and This New Star, This **2nd Sun(Rise)** as "**Mother**", as **Children of the Light. Itym & Ivy** sat and watched as a Garden filled with birds, bees, flowers and trees. He and She sat and watched as these **2 Lights** together commanded this Earth to bring forth Life, and herb's bearing seeds after their kind and fruit trees bearing fruit after their kind. They then sat and watched as this **2nd Sun(Rise)** faded into the night sky, **IY** said "Our **Sun(Set)** shall be with you always" but this **2nd Sun(Rise),** She will return every 2000 years to Judge the Hearts of Man on what he is teaching Her Children, the children of Mother Earth. **IY** said "This day shall be forever known as(fka) "**Saturday**" **(Sat Today)** a day to Sat, Rest & Pray. Remember it also as the **Sabbath, the 7th day** of Time the day you should **Sat & Bathe** in the glory of my Name and Prepare for Her Return." After **IY** had created all the great beasts on the land and in the sea,

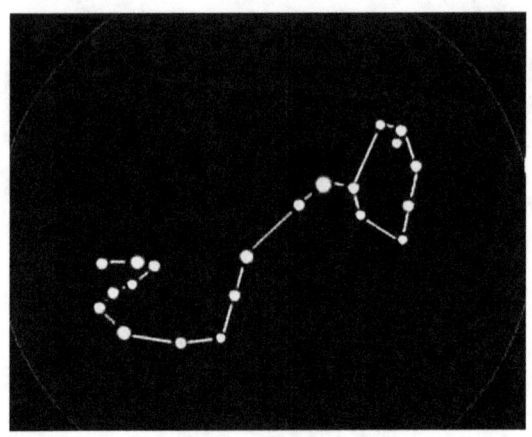

Scorpion

IY created every winged bird in the sky, **IY** created every living creature on this Earth, things you can see and things you cannot. Then **IY** blessed them, and **IY** said to them, "Be fruitful, and multiply, plenish this Earth and give a name every beast that you subdue". The Tree shall have dominion over this **Earth,** over the beast of the land, the fish in the sea and over Every winged creature in the sky. After all that was made was made **IY** commanded them to take a branch from the Tree of Life for protection. Learn to become the Greatest **Archer** on this **Earth,** giving him power over the beast of this Earth and use its power to protect future generations to come. Use it to bring peace to this wild and savage land, they call "**Yit**" to honor woman as the life force of this planet. **Itym** knew that only with the Power given to the Tree will Peace ever be maintained so **Itym** and **IY** made a Covenant. A Promise Never to use this branch from the Tree of Life to kill another human being. **Itym and Ivy** grew to be Giants in this One Land they call **Yit.**

The Book of Spiritual Solution: He, She and the Tree

This branch was 12 foot long and as Black as the night a Tree that looked burnt but not burnt with a Y at its top. Every One Thousand years He and She lived on This Earth equaling only one day to **This Light**. So every **2000 years, Itym, Ivy** & their descendants would watch the rising of this **2nd Sun(Rise)** just as **IY** had promised, judging the heart of All Mankind. For 6000 years, He and She with the Power of the Tree continued to walk as Giants upon this Earth giving names to all of the beast that they had conquered, walking among them as King of All Beast. And there was Peace on Earth, **IY** then commanded **Itym** to write mankind's history past, present and future in the Stars. Creating The Original Book of Time filled with the Constellation. Connecting every star for the first time. The First Book to teach the Children of all future generations who we are and where we come from. However, **IY** saw it as the **7th day**, and **Itym** had grown tired.

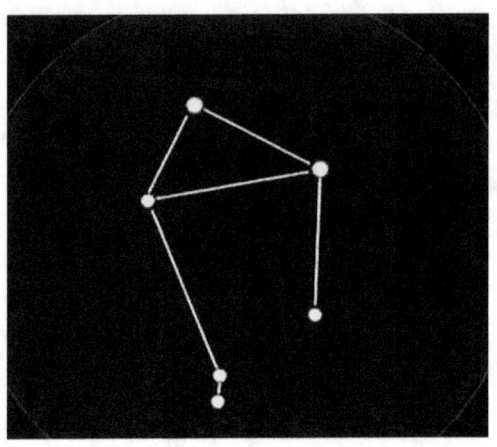

Scales

IY decided it had come time for him to rest. So **IY** sent a **Scorpion** to bite Itym, putting him into a deep sleep so that on the 7th day he would rest. For 3 days, he laid in a coma as his spirit teetered on the Scales between Life and Death. Weighing the earthly burdens of his heart against the feather, a load he had carried for 6000 years, and for 3 days, the world was in mourning as their world was casted into darkness. The people of "**Yit**" thought their King was dead. The children of the time built Monuments to **Itym** to resemble The Great Mountain, this Man who had lived for thousands of years. Honoring This King of Kings by aligning these monuments to mirror the image written of himself in the stars. His body was taken back atop the Great Mountain Birthplace of "**He, She and The Tree**". Naming his burial site as the Mound of Ever Rest calling these Mountains "The Place where the Him is laying". On the 3rd day, the **Virgin Lily** was sent to preserve the seed of Itym Blowing the Breath of Life back into Man resurrecting him from his dead like sleep.

Taking into herself the Spirit of Man & The Cosmic Consciousness of the **I & the Y.** She immaculately conceived a child. As a gift from Infinity the virgin was given a stone containing the **Wisdom of the Ages** past, present and future. And on this return of the **2nd Sun(Rise) New King** was born a giant of a man. Born with the height and strength to bend this 12ft branch into a Bow as **Itym** did in the beginning. Bestowing onto him the **Staff of Kings** and **Infinity's Virgin Stone.** The people overwhelmed with joy built a great monument facing the **Lion** constellation to honor their **New King** and the divine story written in the night sky. But as time passed men begin to separate himself from other men marking the beginnings of their prejudices and discrimination toward another human being. Declaring all albinos banish and to go live on the **Great Mountain**. The human race started moving further and further away from the ways **IY** had set before them, slowly overtime mankind began to lose their height & statue. When **IY** looked down into the heart of man, **IY** saw that his heart has started down the twisted road of discrimination.

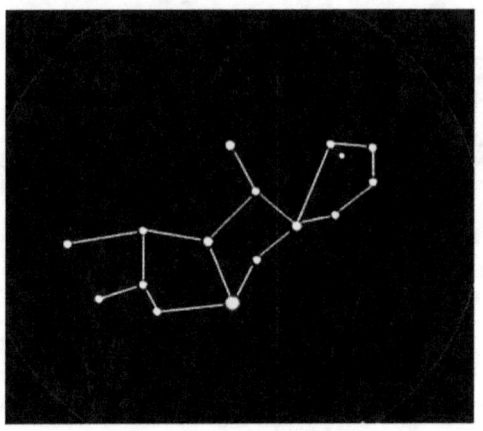

Virgin

The people became lazy and not wanting to work the land themselves told these albinos "We made you, you will work the land for us", forcing them into slavery. After a time, this **race of albino's** refuse to work the land and they revolted. When they revolted the people said "If they will not work the land, use the power within the tree to kill them all". The king refused, he remembered the covenant between **Itym** and **IY**, the power within the tree should never use to kill another human being. The time had come again for the Rising of the **2nd Sun** but this time **This Light** was a greater than all the past Lights. A Light so bright it looked as though a planet had exploded. **IY** said to the King, "The end of all Flesh has come". The tongue and the heart have of man become evil and the land is filled with violence and jealousy. **IY** must destroy this evil and all those who do not remember This Story". **IY** then commanded the King to build an Ark and take the Covenant into the Ark to keep this 12 ft pole/staff safe. He summoned his wisest Kings and commanded them to bring him a male and a female of all the animals on this Earth.

It had been decided that **IY** would destroy this evil to separate man because of color and create a **New Earth**. After gathering all the animals his family and his earthly treasures including the Virgin Stone, the king board the ark. Then **IY** sent down the rain and flooded The Land of **"Yit", the First Super Iyland** once a beautiful Paradise. Sinking **Yit** to the deepest depths of the sea leaving the **Crabs** to eat away the evil left at the bottom of the sea. **IY** said "**IY** will raise this land back up to form 7 New Lands and may the Rainbow serve as a message to future generations that "**All Colors Can Live Together**". And as the waters receded **Mother Earth gave birth to 7 New Lands and 7 New Seas**. The 7 Lands as her daughters and the 7 seas as her sons. Each land beginning and ending with an "A" in remembrance of The Great Mountain and the Pyramids they had left behind; **AsiA, AropA, AfricA, AmAricA, AtlAntiA, AustrAliA & AntArcticA** to be a generational reminder of where we come from. The people of 3 Lands **Asia, Aropa and Africa** lived in peace for thousands of years as a Tri-Nation. These people of many different colors were united not by the color of their skin but this time by the color of their hair.

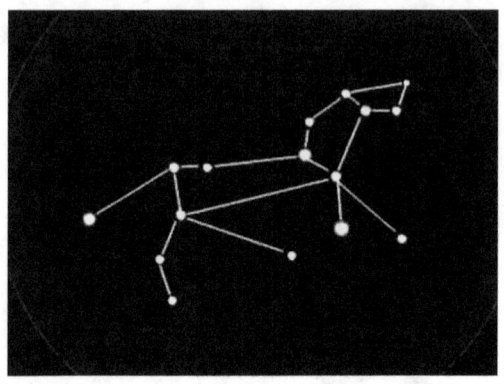

Lion

Their hair was black as the branch from the Tree of Life and atop this 12ft pole waved a flag striped with a **Rainbow of Colors Red, Black, Green, Yellow and White representing The Colors of Humanity.** This piece of Tree of Life was passed down to future generations as a **Emblem of Millions** of Years of Peace. **Red** is for the **Blood** of the Human Race, **Black** for the **Tree** of Life, the Tree that looked burnt but not burnt **Green** for the Mother **Earth, Yellow** for the **Sun** & **White** for the Living Light of Infinity. These 3 lands were **Asia as the Father Land, Africa as the Mother Land, and Aropa as a Baby Land (Babylon)**. These 3 Lands were rule by **Gin** the **Yellow King & Isys his Black Queen** who kept the Gin Stone & the Staff of Kings as their prize possession. It was foretold that out of the Caucasus Mountain a tribe of pale skin golden haired people would come to be forever known as (fka) Caucasians. These golden-haired people found the mountains of **Asia** too hard to climb. These golden-haired people found the sands of Africa too soft to cross. When these golden-haired people said, "We come from The Great Mountain", the people of **Aropa** welcomed them with open arms as they waved a white flag, a flag unfamiliar to the black-haired people of **Aropa** so they took it as a Sign of Peace.

Over time, "**Aropa**" changed its name to "**Europa**" as a Joint Sign of Peace between these 2 People. Then a **Great War** broke out between these 2 people because the child of Queen of the golden-haired people was born with dark skin and golden hair. The original people of Aropa were forced from their land and into the sea, sailing west toward the setting sun to **Amarica** and some east toward the rising sun to **Australia**. Those who stayed later would form **Arabia**. **Gin** made a final stand to not allow this evil to cross the sea by use the Tree of Life turning it from a Guidon of Peace into a Weapon of War. Everything on the land and in the sea died forming a Dead Sea. This breaking of the Covenant was a turning point, the downfall in history that cursed future generations into mortal slavery. **Gin** vowed that his Spirit would watch over the land and its people till the day the name **Aropa** rise from a long forgotten past and take her place with her sisters at their round table we call "Earth". The Tree of Life now broken into 2~6 feet staffs were picked up by the Twins of **Gin and Isys, (Shiva and Shiba)**

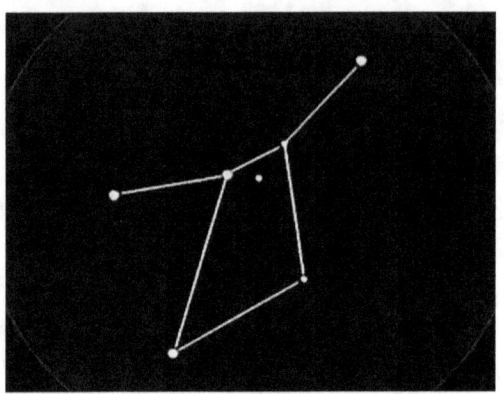

Crab

Blessing with a mark upon their forehead, **IY** told them "Go, no man can harm you, give one to Asia and the other to **Africa** teach her children this story of the **First He, the First She and the First Tree**". Use the power within the tree to leverage great walls to defend your lands from this evil to enslave another human. As **Shiva** ventured deep into **Asia,** he took a wife passing on to her the Virgin Stone, and the all-seeing eye spreading stories throughout the land of the **Great War** and the power within the staff that he possessed. The power to destroy worlds and the power to create new ones. As **Shiba** with her 6 ft staff ventured into **Africa** marking the boundary lines for the land of future **Kings & Queens of Shiba**. The branch now a 6 ft long staff held by the Kings of Egypt serving as the **Emblem of Millions of Years** of History, using the **Ankh** as the symbol of the infinite **Unity of He, She and the Tree**. Identifying the **Apis Bull** in the night sky as their New Age of Enlightenment with new kings and new gods. Upon the Rising of the **2nd Sun(Rise)** stories were being told that the Spirit of Gin had been captured and it had been placed in a Lamp for all times.

The people soon forgot that Gin ever existed. Building idols to their New **King Osiris and his Queen Isys** bowing down to them as gods here on Earth. Condemned to building new idols to new gods becoming idol worshipers. Over time the worship of the **Apis Bull** & many other gods became a common practice in the lives of these slaves. The Branch from the Tree of Life stayed in Egypt for thousands of years untouched and long forgotten. **IY** said "This is not good", Man had not only enslaved man's body to do all his work but had also enslaved his mind that there was many other gods. As It has been foretold that there will come a man, a deliverer who would free the people from under the oppressive rule of Ramses of Egypt and into a Promised Land, telling the people that there is only One God and it lived on the **Great Mountain** and it calls itself **"IY(eye) AM"**. So **IY** send a man who had walked among kings to get the Tree take it out of Egypt this 6 ft staff, a piece of the Tree of Life that was burnt but not burnt. **IY** commanded him to follow this New Star and to take the Tree and Set the people Free.

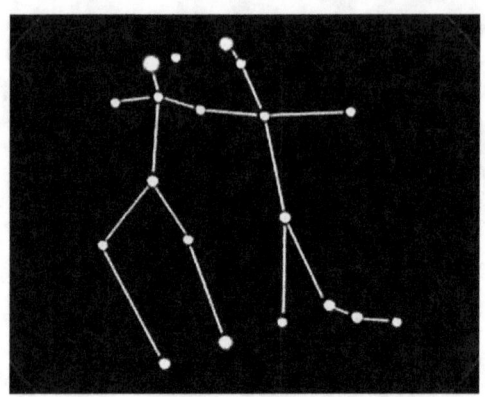

Twins

Leading the people to the base of the **Great Mountain** sparing them from the wrath of the Divine Light. Sounding the Rams Horn of Freedom setting their souls free from the bondage of mortal slavery. **IY AM** the way, the truth and the Living Light of Infinity saying **"IY AM** shall be **My Name For Infinity**, let it serve as a Memorial to All Future Generations". Climbing to the top of the Great Mountain, he brought back **12 commands meant** for future generations carved onto a piece of petrified wood from the Ark.

Commandments 1

IY(eye)AM the Living Light that lead you out of the land of Egypt and out of the house of bondage.

Do you believe that **IY AM** that Living Light that lead your ancestors out of bondage?

Commandment 2

You will have no other god before or after Me.

Know Me as "**IY AM**"

Do you call any man alive or dead your God?

Commandment 3

You will not make any graven image, or any likeness of anything that is in heaven above, No graven image of anything on this Earth or below the waters of this Earth.

Do you worship the graven image of a dead man on a cross or the tombs of the dead?

Commandment 4

You will not bow down yourself to anyone for any reason nor serve anyone for any reason, **IY will punish the Fathers** of the children, of the third and fourth generation of **anyone** that is jealous **(envy us) of Me**. **IY** will show loving kindness to all of you that **Love Me and Keep My Commandments.**

Do you bow down to serve anyone or anything other than **This Living Light of Truth**?

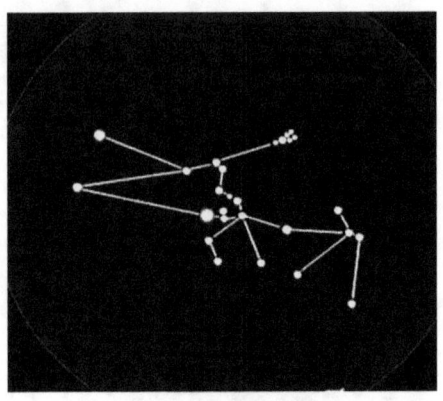

Bull

Commandment 5

You will not speak **My Name** in vain; **IY** will consider it a sin for those that speaks My Name in vain.

Do you know the name **For Infinity?**

Remember Me as "**IY AM**"

Commandment 6

You will **Remember the First 7 Days of Time** as The First 7 Holydays. For 6 days, you shall labor and do all your work; but on the **7th day you will not labor** or do any work. **IY** said "This 7th day of Time shall be forever known as (fka) "**Saturday** ", the **Sabbath Day**. Always Remember it as the day **IY** gave you to **Sat, Rest and Pray**. Observing this day as the **Sabbath Day** and within this day you are to **Sat & Bathe in the Glory of My Name**.

No soul within the gates of your home, no one within the four walls of your house will do any work, for in this 7th day **IY** created all the Heavens and Earth and Rested

Do you honor the 7th day as **Saturday** the day to **Sat, Rest & Pray** and the **Sabbath day to Sat & Bathe** in the Glory in the name **IY AM**

Commandment 7

You will **Honor** your **Father** and your **Mother** that your days may be long in this Land in which **IY** have given you.

Do you Acknowledge and Honor your Father and Mother?

Commandment 8

You will not kill.

Have you ever killed anyone's spirit?

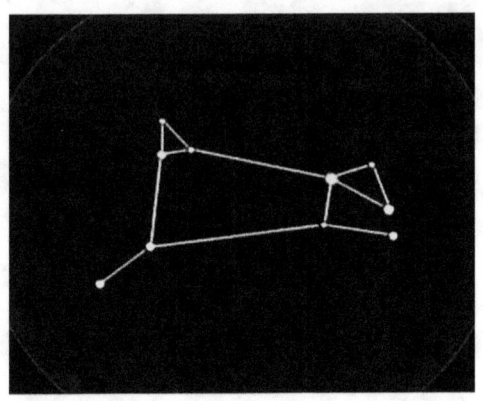

Ram

Commandment 9
    You will not forget the Adults not in your Family Tree
    Do you Remember your Family Tree as well as your Adult Tree?
    Have you forgotten where you come from

Commandment 10
    You will not steal.
    Have you ever taken anything from anyone without asking?

Commandment 11
    You will not bear false witness against your neighbor.
    Have you ever twisted the truth for self-gratification or personal profit?

Commandment 12

You will not be jealous of your neighbors house or your neighbors spouse, your neighbors wife or your neighbors life or anything that is that of your neighbor's

Are you jealous of anyone or anything someone else has in his or her possession?

When he tried to show the people This Story written in the Heavens, but they could not see it so they did not believe it. This stiff-necked group of people refused to look up to see that **IYAM** Infinity so they stayed slaves to the old ways. These 12 Commands meant to serve as rules to help guide the human heart and to know these 4 letters in the name "**IYAM**. Time approach again for the Rising of the **2nd Sun(Rise)**. The **Staff of Shiba** was passed down through time from the hands of Kings into the hands of slaves and finally into the hands of a young carpenter name Jesus calling his shepherd staff "the Staff of Ages". He would tell them stories of the Tree giving them a renewed Faith a heartfelt peace from within.

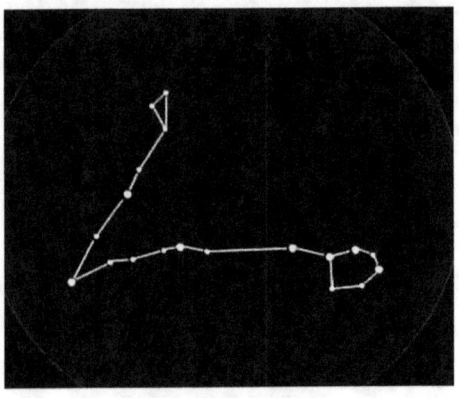

2-Fish

He went out and found **2 Fish**ermen teaching them of the **2 Fish** written in the night sky. Telling the people of Our Fathers whose art that lives in the heavens. With **Itym**, Our First Father Waving Peace on Earth with the Tree of Life. He said "**IY(eye) AM** is the Alpha and the Omega, The Beginning and the end are all existent. When the people started believing what he was saying the church plotted to kill him. Not knowing that the shepherd staff that he carried was the Staff of the Moses. Leaving the people with **2 more commands meant** for the children of the tomorrow.

Commandment 1-You should love the **Living Light** with all of your heart, with all of your soul and with all of your mind.

Do you love this **Living Light** with all your heart your soul and your might?

Commandment 2-You should do onto others as you would have them do unto you.

Do you treat people the way you want to be treated?

He continued to go around saying, "This Story of **He, She & the Tree** is written in the heavens for all to see. Watch the heavens for a **2nd Sun(Rise)** is coming. The stories of him feeding multitudes of people with just **2 Fish** spread throughout the land. His stories had started pulling the people out of the churches as they stated looking into the night skies at these **2 Fish**. Soon they stop going to church, the church knew this could not continue. The church put him on trial, and was repeatedly asked "Who is this Almighty Father", he repeatedly replied "as Time is My Father, Nature is My Mother now and they are "**IY(eye)AM**". The church said he was calling Himself "God" and they found him guilty of heresy. So they tied him to his shepherd staff and impaled him. When the wisemen came from the east looking for the **Staff of Queen Shiba**, they ask "Where is the one with the **Staff of Kings** that you proclaim "**King of the Jews**" and predicted the coming of **this new star**. They replied "He is dead they impaled him, you will find him on the road to Rome, he is the one with a shepherd **staff** tied **across** his back.

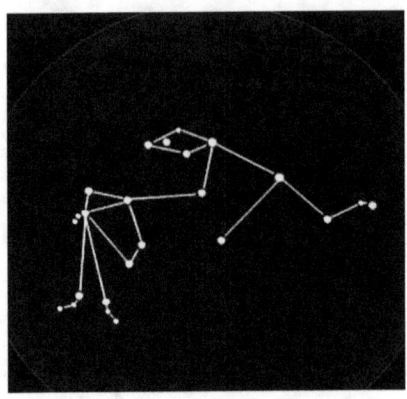

Water Bearer

When the wisemen told church that in their story, it wasn't a sling that defeated Goliath but was a javelin, the **Staff of Queen Shiba** that was pass down as **King Solomons Rod and the Staff of Moses** that they had tied to the back saying "since he lived with the staff let him die with the staff" so they buried him with it when they went to his tomb, they found the staff and his body was gone. The church then changed this Story into his story proclaiming him as the son of God, here on Earth hoping to keep the trees power a secret. Stories that the Staff they call the **Spear of Destiny** was in Africa. A king in the 5th century from the land now known as Europe dispatched his army of knights to retrieve the **Spear of Destiny**. They were met by the African King Zulu a descendent of the lost tribe of Lot. He stood over 7 feet tall with skin as dark as the night and wearing no clothes, beckoning "If you want it, come get it." As the battle began, they soon learned his skills with this 6ft lance was extra ordinary as if it had a life force of its own. The invading King in fear of losing used his new sword against King Zulus mighty staff, breaking the spear and this mighty sword in half, and as King Zulu lashed the broken blade to one of his now 2-3ft spears double its extraordinary power.

The Book of Spiritual Solution: He, She and the Tree

With these 2 short spears, this one man battled for 6 straight days against this invading army honoring the **7th day as the day of Rest**, he lay down his spears and rested. To prevent future European from invading Africa a Peace Treaty between Africa and Europe was made that one half the Tree would stay in Africa, and the other half would go back to Europe. While there they taught these Europeans **Outline of Mankind's Timeline Written in the Stars of First He, the First She and the Very First Tree,** soon we will be entering into a new age the Age of this Water bearer that is pouring the stars as living water into the Cup Constellation now overflowing with the knowledge of the stars for all the world to look up and see, along with stories of the lance of Lots descendent, that was the actual branch from the Tree of Life that has never lost a battle. Then in the 6th century a King from the Land of Arabia with his Army of Knights invaded Europe to take this Staff of the Ages back to the Holy Land where it stayed for 500 years. Until in the 11th Century, a new Army of Knights wearing the sign of a cross invaded the Holy Land found the Staff of Moses, this Rod of Solomon and wanted to used its power to control Europe.

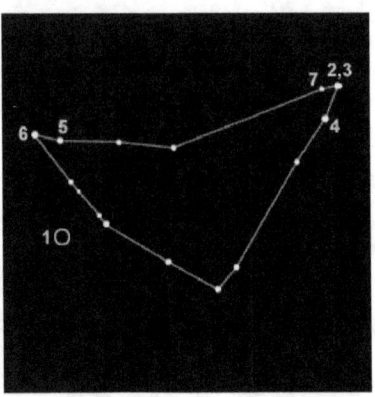

Eye of Infinity

Thinking they could control the world with it, in 1400 they brought it here to Amarica, the New World, hoping to control its people. Word of the people from the north had come not to enslave them but to kill, not just the body but their whole ideology. After years of killing these foretold invaders, they carved head of these invaders so that the future generations of Amarica would know his face. Century's later these same European came back to Amarica after the church learn that their piece of the **Cross of Jesus** was now in the New World. Then in the late 18th century these Europeans return to Africa to steal that piece of the **Staff of Kings** that they left centuries before. Bribing a tribesman to poison Shaka, King of the Zulu nation and to steal his spear, Africa's piece of the Tree of Life. Secretly taking the Tree back to Europe hoping to unlock its Power. It is the Will of Infinity that the children of the 21st-century understand these letters that has been passed down through time, these letters are the characters that form the basis of our spoken word of the past. We are now entering a **Age of the Water Bearer**, a new Age of Enlightenment. The **Wisdom of the Ages** that is written with the stars.

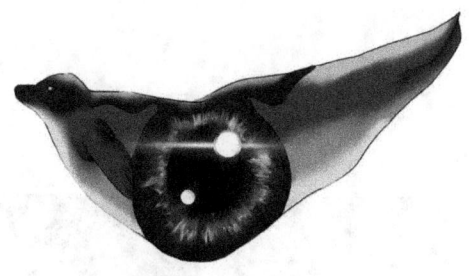

This story came to me one day when I had a dream that I was floating in space and all the constellations were being drawn right in front of me but when it came around to the constellation Capricorn, I didn't see a goat, I was looking at a **Giant Cosmic Eye**. As I stepped throughout this **Cosmic Eye**, I found I had **No Feet, No Hands and No Body**. When I looked out into the void of space, I saw **12 Suns** circling a **Light**. A **Light** so hypnotic that I couldn't take my eyes off it than it began to grow and in a flash the **Light** consumed me. I look again to see **12 Galaxies s**piraling this same **Light** in a flash I'm looking at **12 Universes** than **12 Megaverses.** Flashing to the point where my mind just couldn't take it anymore then everything came to a complete stop and I found myself falling back to **Earth** but as I'm falling, I see a **13th** Star circling the **12** Suns then the **IY** placed in my mind this story of mankind written with the Stars for the whole world to see as a new science call **Histrology** the **History of Religion explained to the Science of Astrology** building a **Bridge connecting Science and Religion. Before** the beginning & **After** the end of time they will always be "**Infinity.**

www.ingramcontent.com/pod-product-compliance
Lightning Source LLC
LaVergne TN
LVHW020448080526
838202LV00055B/5383